Usborne Fairy Tales for Bedtime

Retold by Rosie Dickins

Illustrated by Nathalie Ragondet

Contents

Cinderella

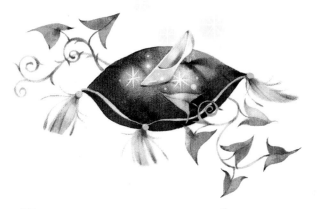

O nce upon a time, there was
a beautiful young girl named
Ella. But everyone called
her Cinderella...

...because while the rest of her family slept in soft feather beds, she had to huddle by the fireplace in the kitchen and wake covered in ash and cinders.

Cinderella's mother had died years before, and her father (who was rarely home) had married again. His new wife made Cinderella scrub and sweep and cook and clean. But she lavished every luxury on her own two girls – who were as ugly as Cinderella was beautiful.

One day, an invitation arrived which made Cinderella's stepmother shriek with excitement.

"The prince is holding a ball!" she cried. "And we're invited." At once, she and her daughters began discussing dresses and shoes, and how to impress a prince.

"Please may I go too?" begged Cinderella.

"You?" laughed her stepmother. "Just look at you, covered in cinders like a kitchen maid! They'd never let *you* into the palace."

Over the following days, Cinderella's stepmother summoned the most fashionable dressmakers and hairdressers, to make the ugly sisters look slightly less ugly. It wasn't easy.

Finally, the big night arrived. The sisters and their mother left in a swish of finery, and Cinderella was alone in an empty house.

"I *wish* I could go to the ball," she sighed. Hardly had the words left her lips than there was a tap at the door. There stood an old lady leaning on a silver stick. Cinderella had never seen her before, but she seemed to know Cinderella.

"Hello dear," she said. "I'm your fairy godmother and you *shall* go to the ball! First, you need a coach. Can you bring me a pumpkin?"

Cinderella was too astonished to ask why. She ran to pick a pumpkin from the garden.

Her godmother waved the stick. There was a shower of stars, so bright that Cinderella had to blink. When she looked again, the pumpkin had become a round, golden coach. She gasped.

"Now the coachman and horses," her godmother went on. "I think you'll find a lizard and four mice in the garden..." Another wave, and there was a coachman dressed all in green, and four handsome white horses.

"And your dress," she added. With a final wave, Cinderella's ragged old clothes became a glittering ballgown, while delicate glass slippers sparkled on her feet.

Cinderella spun around in delight. "Oh thank you, godmother," she cried.

"Now remember," said her godmother, as Cinderella stepped into the golden coach. "My magic will wear off at midnight. You must leave before then!"

"I will," promised Cinderella.

The palace was ablaze with lights when Cinderella arrived. As she entered, a hush fell. No one had ever seen anyone so beautiful. Shyly, the prince came over and asked her to dance. Cinderella's glass slippers tinkled lightly on the dance floor as she and the prince whirled and twirled together.

They were having so much fun, she almost forgot her godmother's warning – until a clock began to strike...

"Midnight!" she gasped. She gathered up her skirts and dashed for the door.

"Don't go," called the prince, racing after her. But he was too late. She had vanished – except for one sparkling glass slipper. Gently, he picked it up.

"I'm going to find the girl who fits this," he announced boldly. "And then I'm going to ask her to marry me!"

The very next day, the prince and his servants carried the slipper from house to house. Everyone tried it, from haughty princesses to humble house maids, but it would fit no one.

Cinderella's ugly sisters tried it too, but their feet were far too big and clumpy. Then a shy, cinder-covered figure stepped forward.

"It can't be *hers*," sneered the sisters. "She wasn't even at the ball."

"I want *everyone* to try," insisted the prince, gazing hopefully at the girl. Was it his imagination, or was there something familiar about her...? He held his breath as, daintily, she lifted her foot. The slipper was a perfect fit!

"I knew I'd find you," he cried joyfully, sweeping Cinderella into his arms.

"My prince," she laughed, hugging him right back.

At that moment, there was a tap at the door. It was Cinderella's fairy godmother. "Time for a little more magic," she said, with a smile.

She waved her wand and Cinderella's dusty dress was transformed into a dazzling wedding gown – and there was a golden coach to carry the smiling couple back to the palace, where they lived happily ever after.

Cinderella's stepmother and sisters were less happy. "It's all your fault," the stepmother grumbled at her daughters, "for having such big feet!"

Goldilocks and the Three Bears

Goldilocks had pretty golden curls
and a sweet-as-sugar smile. She
looked like an angel. Unfortunately,
she didn't behave like one...

"Greedy Goldilocks," her mother sighed, as she caught her in the kitchen. "Those cakes are for later! Put them back. Why don't you play outside?" she went on. "Just don't go into the forest. It's full of bears!"

Goldilocks didn't answer. She was already dancing out of the door. Leaves rustled and birds sang as she skipped along the path to the forest. "I can't see any bears," she laughed, looking around. Between the trees, she spied a pretty wooden cottage.

"Who lives here?" she wondered, skipping up to the door. *Rat-a-tat-tat!* No one came, so she pushed her way in.

"Ooh, something smells good," she thought. On a table sat three bowls of creamy porridge.

Goldilocks grabbed the biggest bowl and scooped up a steamy spoonful. "Oof!" she spluttered. "Too hot." She reached for the middle-sized bowl. "Ugh! Too cold." But the littlest bowl was... "*Mmm, just right.*" Goldilocks gobbled it all up.

Beside the table were three painted wooden chairs. Goldilocks clambered onto the biggest chair. "Oof, too hard." Next she flopped onto the middle-sized chair. "Ugh, too soft." But the littlest chair was... "*Mmm, just right.*"

At least, it *was* until its little legs gave way beneath her. *CRASH!*

"Ow! Now where will I sit?" she moaned, brushing off the splinters.

A curtain hung across one corner. Behind it stood three comfy-looking beds. She bounced on the biggest bed. "Oof, too hard!" She sank into the middle-sized bed. "Ugh, too soft." But the littlest bed was... "*Mmm*, just right."

Feeling sleepy after all the porridge, she pulled the covers up to her chin and dozed off. She was snoozing so soundly, she didn't hear the door open and three sets of paws come padding inside. But she jolted awake when three voices suddenly boomed out.

"Who's been eating *my* porridge?" growled a big, deep voice.

"Who's been eating *my* porridge?" gasped a middling sort of voice.

"Who's been eating *my* porridge?" squeaked a little baby voice. "And look, they've eaten it all up!"

"*Uh-oh*," thought Goldilocks, peeking around the curtain. "Bears!"

"Who's been sitting in *my* chair?" growled the great big bear.

"Who's been sitting in *my* chair?" gasped the middle-sized bear.

"Who's been sitting in *my* chair?" squeaked the little baby bear. "Look, they've broken it!"

The three bears turned towards the beds... Goldilocks dived under the covers, trembling. "I hope they don't see me!"

"Who's been sleeping in *my* bed?" growled the great big bear.

"Who's been sleeping in *my* bed?" gasped the middle-sized bear.

"Who's been sleeping in *my* bed?" squealed the little baby bear. "Look, she's still in it!"

Goldilocks shrieked and flung off the bedcovers. She raced out of the cottage and all the way home, as fast as her legs could carry her. And she was never, or *almost* never, naughty again.

Jack and the Beanstalk

There was once a poor boy
named Jack whose mother
sent him to market to sell
their cow.

So off Jack strolled, leading the cow, when he bumped into a stranger.

"That's a fine animal," said the stranger, patting the cow's milky-white flank. "I'll give you a handful of beans for her."

"Beans?" laughed Jack. "She's worth more than that!"

"Ah, but these are magic beans," promised the man, winking. And somehow, Jack found himself nodding...

"Silly boy," cried his mother when he got back. "Now we have no cow and no money!" She flung the beans out of the window and went sadly to bed.

The next morning, Jack woke to find his room flooded with green light. Leaves and tendrils filled the window. "A giant beanstalk!" he gasped, gazing up. The end disappeared into the clouds.

"I wonder what's up there?" thought Jack – and he began to climb. Up and up, until the ground dropped away and his cottage looked like a toy. Up into the clouds...

The beanstalk ended outside a towering castle, with its huge oak door ajar. Jack slipped through.

Inside stood a table and chair as big as
a house. A whole tree was burning in the
fireplace, and a whole ox was roasting over it.

"This must be a giant's castle!" Jack gasped.
The floor began to shake. "Uh-oh, footsteps."
He ducked behind a table leg.

"*Fee-fi-fo-fum*," roared the giant, stomping
in. "I smell the blood of a little man." He licked
his lips greedily. "And
I *eat* little men for
breakfast!"

Behind the table,
Jack shivered. The
giant looked around
but didn't spy him.
So he grabbed the ox
instead, and crunched
it up in two bites.

"Now, where's that hen?" he muttered. He picked up a basket and roughly shook it, until a hen with shining golden feathers fell out.

"Lay!" he snapped. With much flapping and fluttering, the hen laid a heavy golden egg.

"Wow," thought Jack. "That's real gold!"

"Where's my harp?" the giant went on. He opened a cupboard and yanked out a harp with shining golden strings. "Play!" And the harp began to play all by itself. It played such a sweet, restful tune that the giant was soon snoring peacefully.

"What treasures," thought Jack. "If we had those, Mother would never be short of money again."

Quickly, quietly, Jack tiptoed over and seized the hen and the harp. But as he crept away, he stumbled and the harp let out a loud *twang.* "Oh no!"

Behind him came an ear-splitting roar. The giant had woken up.

Jack didn't hesitate. He raced to the beanstalk and slid down as fast as he could, the giant clambering clumsily after him.

As soon as Jack reached the bottom, he seized a hatchet and chopped through the stalk. The giant was only halfway down. He fell to earth with a giant-sized thump, and that was the end of him.

But Jack and his mother lived happily with the golden hen and the golden harp and, as they soon had lots of golden eggs to sell, they never wanted for anything again.

Rapunzel

Once upon a time, a young mother fell ill. Only one thing could cure her – a herb named rapunzel.

But it was cold midwinter and there was none to be had, except in the garden of a wicked witch. Bravely, her husband crept into the garden to pick a leaf...

As the stem snapped, he heard a shriek. "Stop, thief!" It was the witch. "How dare you steal my plant? You shall pay with your life!"

"I'm sorry," he pleaded. "It was for my wife, she's very ill. Please, she's expecting a baby..."

The witch gave a nasty grin. "I'll take the baby as payment then."

Sadly, the man bowed his head. He had no choice. The witch was too powerful.

The baby, when she came, was a beautiful rosy-cheeked girl. She had scarcely drawn her first breath when there was a rap at the door.

The witch had come to claim her. "I'll call her Rapunzel," she cackled, as she took the tiny bundle away, "in memory of our bargain."

So Rapunzel grew up with the witch – who guarded her jealously. She kept her locked in a tower with no door. The only way in or out was to climb, but the sides of the tower were as slippery as glass and cruel thorn bushes grew all around.

Rapunzel had thick, golden hair which grew and grew, and was never cut. When the witch came, she would call up: "Rapunzel, Rapunzel, let down your hair."

Then Rapunzel would let her hair tumble to the ground, and the witch would climb up it.

One day, a prince was riding by the tower when he spied Rapunzel, combing her hair by her window. She was so beautiful, he lost his heart to her in an instant. And Rapunzel, who had never seen a man before, was equally charmed.

Quickly, she let down her hair. Boldly, the prince climbed up. They talked and laughed for hours. And by sunset, they had vowed to marry.

"But you must leave before the witch comes," warned Rapunzel. "Or she'll kill you."

"I'll be back soon," promised the prince. "And then we'll escape together!"

When the witch returned, she sniffed suspiciously. "A man has been here," she hissed. "But you won't see him again!" She chopped off Rapunzel's beautiful hair and locked her in a cupboard. And then the witch waited...

Before long, there came a whisper. "Rapunzel, Rapunzel, let down your hair." The golden tresses tumbled down and the prince climbed up – only to find the witch holding the other end.

"You'll never see your darling again," she cackled, holding up a claw-like hand and mouthing a spell. The prince's world suddenly grew dark. The witch had blinded him. Then he felt her cold fingers on his chest, trying to push him back out of the window.

"No," he cried, thinking of the deadly drop onto the thorns below. He fought blindly, and managed to throw the witch off balance...

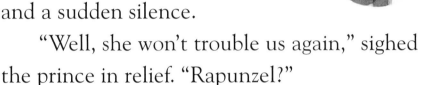

She teetered...

     and tottered...

and fell through the window herself. There was a loud shriek – and a sudden silence.

"Well, she won't trouble us again," sighed the prince in relief. "Rapunzel?"

"Here," answered a soft voice. The prince felt his way over to the cupboard and unlocked it, and Rapunzel rushed into his arms. Tears of joy streamed down her cheeks – and when her tears touched the prince's eyes, he found he could see again.

He blinked and smiled. "We're free," he told her gently. "Come with me, and we can live happily ever after together."

And they did.

Puss in Boots

There was once a poor miller's boy who found himself alone in the world, with no family and no job, and only a large stripy cat for company.

The boy's name was Peppo. "Well Puss," he sighed, stroking the cat's soft, tawny fur. "I've no work and almost no money. What will we do together?"

"We will do very well, if you will trust me," purred Puss.

"You can talk!" exclaimed Peppo.

"Oh yes," purred Puss, smiling. "And much more besides. You will soon see, if you will just

buy me a new suit and boots."

So Peppo turned out his pockets... With his last few coins, he bought a little red velvet jacket, with hat and boots – and very handsome Puss looked in them.

Puss then caught a couple of fine, fat rabbits and took them to the King. "A present from the Marquis of Catanza," he mewed.

The next day, he took two gleaming silver salmon. "From the Marquis of Catanza," he mewed again.

On the third day, it was a pair of plump golden pheasants...

"Who is this Marquis who keeps sending me gifts?" asked the King curiously.

"You don't know the Marquis?" gasped Puss. "A man famed for his wit, wisdom and wealth?"

"Er, no," admitted the King. "But I'd love to meet him. Can you bring him to the palace?"

Puss smiled.

"What have you done?" moaned Peppo when Puss returned with the invitation. "I'm no marquis!" He looked sadly at his old, patched clothes. "And I can't meet the King like this."

"Don't worry," said Puss. "I'll come up with something. Why don't you go for a swim in the river while I think about it."

So Peppo went for a swim. While he was splashing in the sunshine, Puss took all his clothes and hid them under a rock. Then he ran to the palace, mewing loudly.

"Help, help! Thieves have attacked the Marquis and stolen his clothes, and thrown him in the river to drown!"

The King immediately sent his soldiers and servants to the rescue, along with a suit of his own clothes for Peppo.

So Peppo arrived at the palace dressed like
a king – and looking as handsome as a king, too.
The King's daughter, Princess Perla, blushed
with delight whenever she saw him.

The King gave a great feast to celebrate
Peppo's visit. After all the food, Puss suggested
they go for a walk. "So you can
see my master's castle,"
he mewed.

"What are you doing?"
hissed Peppo.

Puss just winked and
scampered ahead.

Now, it happened that
there was a castle not far
from the King's palace and
it belonged to a fearsome ogre.

Puss ran straight up to the ogre.

"People say you can change shape," he mewed boldly. "But I don't believe it!"

"Then watch," snarled the ogre. And he turned into a great big grizzly bear. "*Grrrrr!*"

"Not bad," admitted Puss. "But I bet you can't go as small as a mouse."

"Watch," growled the bear, shrinking...

Puss grinned – and pounced.

When the King and Peppo arrived, Puss was calmly cleaning his whiskers. "Welcome to my master's castle," he purred. The King was very impressed.

Now it was Peppo's turn to give a feast. He and Perla danced all night and by morning, they were engaged to be married.

So Peppo and Perla lived happily ever after with Puss by their fireside, and Puss never chased another mouse again, except for fun.

Snow White
and the
Seven Dwarfs

Princess Snow White was
the prettiest child you ever
saw, with hair as black as ebony,
lips as red as roses and skin as
white as snow.

As she grew up, she grew ever more beautiful, while her stepmother, the Queen, grew ever more jealous.

Each day, the Queen gazed coldly into her mirror. "Mirror, mirror, on the wall, who is the fairest of them all?"

"You, my Queen," replied the mirror... until one day it said instead, "Snow White."

The Queen scowled. "*I* must be the fairest," she hissed. And she sent a huntsman to take the princess into the forest and kill her.

But the old huntsman took pity on Snow White and left her unhurt among the trees. "Don't go home," he warned, "or the Queen will have you killed."

"Where shall I go?" she wondered sadly.

After much walking, she came to a cottage. There was no one at home, but inside stood seven little beds in a row, and a long, low table set for seven dinners.

By now she was so tired, she crept in and fell asleep by the fire – and that is how the seven dwarfs who lived in the cottage found her, when they came home.

The dwarfs were very surprised to find Snow White, and even more surprised to hear her story. "You poor thing," they cried. "You must stay here with us. You can mind the house while we go out to work, and we will have dinner together each evening."

"Oh, thank you," sighed Snow White.

"Be careful though," warned the dwarfs. "Your stepmother may come after you, even here. Don't let anyone in while we're away!"

Meanwhile, the Queen was gazing into her mirror again. "*Now* who is the fairest?"

"Oh Queen, you are fair, indeed it's true, But Snow White is fairer still than you."

"But she's dead!" wailed the Queen, with a scowl. "Isn't she?"

In reply, the mirror showed her a picture of Snow White and the dwarfs, sitting happily down to dinner.

The Queen howled. "That lying huntsman! I'll have to kill her myself."

The next morning, Snow White had barely cleared the breakfast things when there was a tap at the door. She opened it a crack and saw an old woman.

"Pretty things to buy," croaked the woman, holding up a glittering silver belt.

"I can't let anyone in," said Snow White.

"Then come outside," said the woman.

Snow White didn't want to be rude, so she stepped out. The woman slipped the belt around her waist and pulled, hard. Snow White gasped and fell to the ground, unable to breathe.

When the dwarfs came home, she was still lying there. Quickly, they loosened the belt, and Snow White coughed and sat up.

"Next time, don't even open the door," they told her.

The next day, there was another tap. "I can't open the door," said Snow White.

"Then open the window," came the reply.

Snow White did – and saw an old woman holding out a silver comb. "Try it, dearie."

It looked so pretty, Snow White couldn't resist. But as soon as she touched it, she fell to the floor, for it was poisoned.

When the dwarfs came home, they pulled it away, and Snow White sat up. "Don't accept *anything* from anyone," they said sternly.

The next day, someone tapped again. "Who is it?" Snow White called cautiously.

"Just an old apple-seller."

Snow White peeked out and saw an old woman with a basket of shiny apples.

"These are delicious," she cackled, holding out a glossy green apple with one rosy red cheek. "Look." And she took a bite from the green side.

"It must be all right if *she's* eating it,"
thought Snow White. She took a bite of the
red side – and fell lifeless to the floor. The old
woman threw back her hood and laughed. It
was the Queen, and the red apple was poison.

This time, the dwarfs could not revive
Snow White. With heavy hearts they made a
glass case for her, so as not to hide her beauty,
and left her in a quiet part of the forest.

A few weeks later, a prince was riding by
when he saw Snow White lying peacefully
under the glass, as beautiful as ever. In that
instant, the prince fell utterly in love.

He leaped down, pushed aside the lid and lifted her into his arms. As he stood up, he stumbled over a tree root – and with the jolt, a piece of apple flew out of her mouth.

As soon as the apple passed her lips, the poison ceased to work. Snow White coughed prettily and opened her eyes. She blushed to find herself in the arms of a dashing prince.

"You're alive," he cried happily, while the dwarfs danced around in delight. "Will you marry me?"

"Oh yes," sighed Snow White, blushing even more.

So they were married, and all seven dwarfs came to the wedding.

Hansel and Gretel

H ansel and Gretel lived with their father and stepmother in a little wooden cottage on the edge of an enormous forest.

The forest was so huge and so wild, Hansel and Gretel had never seen most of it. Each morning, their father set off with his hatchet. Each evening, he came home with bundles of firewood to sell. But times were hard and, try as he might, they never had enough to eat.

Late one night, after Hansel and Gretel had gone to bed, their stepmother turned crossly to their father. "If it was just you and me, we might manage," she snapped. "But we can't feed two children as well! You'll have to take them into the forest and leave them."

"No!" cried the woodcutter. But she wouldn't listen. Hunger had hardened her heart. She nagged and bullied, until reluctantly he was forced to agree.

Hansel and Gretel were too hungry and worried to sleep. They had heard every word.

"What now, Hansel?" whispered Gretel.

"Don't worry, I've got a plan," he replied. He waited until everyone was asleep. Then, silently, he slipped outside and filled his pockets with pebbles.

In the morning, the woodcutter hugged his children and gave them each a little piece of bread. "Put on your coats," he said, sighing. "You're coming with me today."

He led them deep into the forest, along strange paths with many twists and turns. At each turn, Hansel lingered and secretly dropped a pebble to mark the way.

"Keep up, son," muttered his father.

Eventually they came to a clearing. "You stay here while I start chopping," said the woodcutter sadly. "I'll come and get you later."

Hansel and Gretel sat and waited. In the distance, they could hear the *thud-thud-thud* of the hatchet. Except it wasn't really a hatchet. The woodcutter had tied a branch so it thudded against a tree when the wind blew.

They sat until the sun began to sink. Gretel shivered. "Time to go home," said Hansel. And back they went, following the pebbles, until they reached the cottage.

"You're home!" cried the woodcutter gladly.

His wife scowled. As soon as the children were in bed, she turned on her husband. "You'll have to try again tomorrow!"

Again, Hansel and Gretel overheard.

"Don't worry," said Hansel. "I'll get some more pebbles." He waited until everyone was asleep, then tiptoed to the door... but it wouldn't open. His stepmother had locked it. "Never mind," he told himself bravely. "I'm sure I can find something else."

The next morning, the woodcutter kissed his children and divided the last little piece of bread between them.

"Put on your coats," he sighed. And off they went, into the forest... This time, Hansel had nothing in his pockets but bread. So he crumbled that, and dropped the crumbs to mark the way.

The woodcutter left them as before – and as before, they sat and waited for the end of the day. Then they got up to make their way home... only to find there were no crumbs to be seen! The forest birds had eaten every one.

"Perhaps I'll remember the way," thought Hansel. But he didn't. They wandered deeper and deeper into the trees, until they stumbled upon a small clearing.

"Look!" gasped Gretel. There, in the middle, stood a little house built of freshly baked gingerbread, with lollipop windows and sugar flowers around the door. It looked wonderful and it smelled even better.

Too hungry to think, they ran over and crammed their mouths with sweet, sticky handfuls. They ate and ate, until they could eat no more. And then they fell asleep.

Gretel was woken by a
sharp prod. It was a witch,
who had built the gingerbread
house to catch passing
children. "Get up, girl," she
snapped. "You're my servant now."

"Hey," called Hansel, trying to stand
up. His head hit something hard. "Ow!"
He was caught in a cage. "Let me out!"

The witch cackled. "You're not going
anywhere. Your sister is going to feed you up,
and then I'm going to eat you!"

Each day, she made Hansel hold out a
finger, so she could feel how fat he was. But he
soon realized that the witch, though powerful,
couldn't see very well. So he would hold out
a twig instead... "Why aren't you fatter?" she
would grumble, leaving him for another day.

One morning, the witch lost patience. "Open the oven," she shouted at Gretel. "The fire is lit and I'm hungry."

Gretel thought fast. "How does it open?"

"Like this, you silly girl," snapped the witch, bending down.

Quick as a flash, Gretel pushed her in and slammed the door – and that was the end of her. Then Gretel opened Hansel's cage and they set out for home, stopping only to fill a basket with gingerbread and take a purse of the witch's gold.

At last, to their delight, they found a familiar path. Then they saw their cottage. Their father was alone inside, for their step-mother had left. "I missed you so much," he sobbed, hugging them tightly.

With the gold, their worries were over – and they all lived happily ever after.

Little Red Riding Hood

Once there was a little girl, whose mother made her a cape and hood of soft, red cloth. She liked the cape so much and wore it so often, everyone began to call her Little Red Riding Hood.

One day, Little Red Riding Hood's mother
asked her to take a cake to her grandmother,
who lived on the other side of the forest.
"Now be careful and stay on the
path," she warned her daughter.
"And don't talk to any wolves!"
Little Red Riding Hood
set off happily. She was so busy
singing to herself and picking
flowers, she didn't notice a dark
shape slinking through the shadows...

In the deepest, darkest part of the forest,
an enormous wolf sprang out in front of her.
"Where are you going, little girl?" he growled.

Little Red Riding Hood was so startled, she
forgot her mother's words. "To visit my granny
beyond the forest," she replied. "I'm taking her
this cake."

The wolf had meant to
eat up Little Red Riding
Hood there and then, but
now he had a better idea.
"I'll eat the old lady first –
and have this little girl and
her cake for dessert!" With
a sly smile, he ran off through
the trees.

The wolf got to the house long before Little
Red Riding Hood. He knocked impatiently on
the door. *Rat-a-tat!*

"Who is it?" called a quavery old voice.

"Your little granddaughter, with a cake for
you," he answered in a squeaky voice.

"Lift up the latch and come in."

The wolf bounded in and swallowed the
grandmother whole – *gulp!*

Then he pulled her frilly cap over his big, hairy ears, tied her shawl around his huge, hairy shoulders, and jumped into her bed.

Soon, there was another knock at the door. *Rat-a-tat!* "Who is it?" quavered the wolf.

"Red Riding Hood, with a cake for you."

"Lift up the latch and come in."

Little Red Riding Hood pushed open the door – and stared. "Granny, what big *ears* you have," she exclaimed.

"All the better to hear you with," squeaked the wolf.

"Granny, what big *eyes* you have."

"All the better to see you with."

"Granny, what big *teeth* you have."

"All the better to eat you with!" snarled the wolf, jumping up and swallowing Little Red Riding Hood and the cake together – *gulp!*

Then the wolf yawned. After eating so much, he felt sleepy. So he flopped down on the bed and closed his eyes.

In a moment, he was snoring loudly – so loudly that a passing woodcutter heard him.

"What a racket," he muttered. "I'd better see if everything is all right."

Quietly, he pushed open the door. As soon as he saw the wolf's bulging belly, he guessed what had happened. "If I'm quick, perhaps I can save whoever's in there," he thought.

He tiptoed over to the bed and picked up a pair of scissors...

Snip, snip! He cut open the wolf's tummy and out sprang Little Red Riding Hood.

Snip, snip! Out tumbled her grandmother too.

"Can you find some stones?" the woodcutter
asked Little Red Riding Hood. He put the stones
in the wolf's tummy and sewed it up. Then they
all crept softly away.

When the wolf woke, his tummy felt peculiar.
"That old granny must have disagreed with me,"
he grumbled. "I'd better drink some water."

He ran to the river, the stones inside him
rattling and rolling with every step. Then he
leaned down to drink... but the stones were
so heavy, he fell right in. *Splosh!* The
rushing water swept him away and
no one ever saw him again.

Little Red Riding Hood and
her granny lived long and happily,
thanks to the brave woodcutter.
And Little Red Riding Hood never,
ever talked to another wolf.

The Elves and the Shoemaker

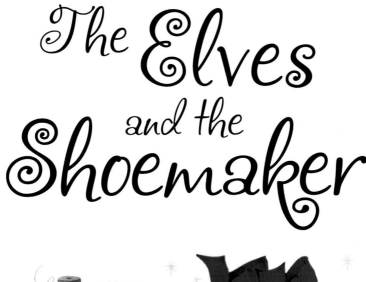

There was once an old shoemaker who fell on hard times. He was so short of money, he couldn't even afford to buy any more leather...

All he had was a few scraps.

"Enough for a small pair," he decided, picking up his scissors. *Snip, snip, snippety-snip.* Carefully, he began to cut out the pieces. By the time he finished, it was too dark to stitch them together.

"I'll do the rest in the morning," he told his wife, yawning. But he never got the chance...

When he woke the next day, the leather had gone! In its place was a pair of shiny new shoes, prettily stitched and polished to perfection.

"Impossible," he thought, rubbing his eyes. But there were the shoes, gleaming in the sunlight. "Look at this," he called to his wife. "Someone finished my shoes last night!"

"Whoever it was, they've done a wonderful job," she exclaimed.

They sold the shoes for a gold coin, and used the money to buy more leather.

"Enough for two pairs," the shoemaker told his wife happily, reaching for his scissors. *Snip, snip, snippety-snip.* By the end of the day, he had cut out the pieces for two tall pairs of boots.

"I'll finish them tomorrow," he said.

But in the morning, there stood two pairs of beautiful new boots, neatly stitched, with bright brass buckles, which he sold for four gold coins...

And so it went on. Each day, the shoemaker bought more leather and cut it out, and each night, someone else stitched it into the most magnificent boots and shoes.

Now the shoemaker's shop was filled with customers, and money poured in. But he still had no idea who was helping him. So one night, he and his wife hid behind a curtain to watch...

They had almost dozed off when the door creaked open. Two ragged little men tiptoed over the threshold. "Elves," breathed the shoemaker, his eyes wide with surprise.

The elves climbed quietly onto the table. Their tiny fingers flashed and flew, until they had stitched and polished a whole row of shiny new shoes and boots. And then they left.

"Poor things," sighed the shoemaker. "Working so hard to help us, when they have nothing but rags themselves."

"Let's make them some new clothes in return," suggested his wife.

The shoemaker nodded.

That day, instead of cutting leather as usual, he made two tiny pairs of elf boots, while his wife sewed two tiny elf suits. At bedtime, they laid their gifts on the table, then hid in the corner and waited...

In the middle of the night, the door creaked again. There was a pitter-patter of tiny footsteps and a squeal of delight. "Look, new clothes!"

The elves put them on at once. When they caught sight of themselves in the mirror, they turned cartwheels for sheer joy. They skipped all around the room, singing:

We look so smart, in our new suits,
Too smart by far, for stitching boots!
Then they danced out of the door, still singing.

The old shoemaker and his wife looked at each other and smiled. They didn't mind losing their magic helpers. Now they had plenty of money and customers, and lots of ideas for new shoes. They were back in business – thanks to the elves.

Aladdin and the Magic Lamp

A laddin was a poor boy, with
no family except his mother.
Or so he thought until, one day,
a man wearing magician's robes
stopped him in the street...

"Aladdin! It's me, Ebenezer."

"Eb-eh-who?" stuttered Aladdin.

The man flashed a toothy smile. "I'm your long-lost uncle. Do as I say and you will make your fortune."

"Well, I could use some money," Aladdin thought. So he followed the man to a lonely mountainside, and watched him mutter some magic words. The ground split open with a noise like thunder. Aladdin shivered.

"Down there is a cave full of treasure," said Ebenezer, pointing. "Take what you like – just bring me the old oil lamp you will find. Hurry!"

Aladdin took a deep breath and climbed down. Slowly his eyes adjusted to the gloom...

He gasped. Before him was a cavern filled with glittering fruit trees. On each tree grew gems of astonishing size and beauty, and on the ground between them lay a battered old brass lamp.

Aladdin crammed his pockets with great bunches of rubies, emeralds and diamonds. Under one tree, he found a carved brass ring, which he slipped onto his finger. Then he picked up the lamp and made his way back.

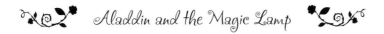

"Pass me the lamp," said Ebenezer, reaching down greedily.

Something in his face made Aladdin wary. "Help me up first," he insisted.

"The lamp!" snarled Ebenezer.

Aladdin shook his head.

"Then stay there and rot!" Ebenezer yelled.

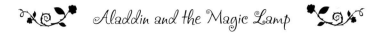

He stamped his foot and the ground closed again, leaving Aladdin alone in the dark.

"What shall I do now?" he wondered. "Um. Maybe I can light this lamp…" He rubbed it on his sleeve. *Kazoom!* A huge, smoky figure appeared. "A genie!" cried Aladdin.

"I am the Genie of the Lamp," boomed the figure. "Your wish is my command."

"Please, take me home," begged Aladdin.

The genie snapped his fingers. Suddenly, Aladdin was outside his mother's house.

"Where did you come from?" she exclaimed. So Aladdin explained… "That magician was a liar," she said, when he had finished. "You don't have an uncle. But he was right about a fortune – look at those gems!"

"The real treasure is the lamp," said Aladdin. "No wonder he wanted it so badly."

Now Aladdin and his mother were no
longer poor. Whatever they wished for, the
Genie of the Lamp would bring. And so they
lived happily – until Aladdin met the
Sultan's daughter, beautiful Princess
Badra, and they fell hopelessly in love.
Aladdin pined and sighed, until his
mother knew she had to do something.

"Let's offer your gems to the Sultan
and ask for Badra's hand in marriage," she said.

The Sultan was very impressed with
the gems. He was less impressed to discover
Aladdin was just an ordinary boy. "How can you
keep my daughter in a manner
fit for a princess?" he boomed.

"Easy," replied
Aladdin, reaching for
the lamp.

Kazoom! The genie floated before him.
"I need a magnificent golden palace..."
The genie snapped his fingers.

Amazed, the Sultan agreed to the wedding
at once. Aladdin and Badra were thrilled.

The celebrations lasted for days and people
came from far and wide to see them. Among
the crowds was the wicked magician Ebenezer.
"That wretched boy must be using the lamp,"
he muttered. "But it won't last. I'll see to that."

He waited until Aladdin had gone out one
day, then took a tray of lamps and stood by the
palace. "New lamps for old!" he called.

Princess Badra leaned out of a window. "Here's an old one," she said, holding up a battered brass lamp. She didn't know about the genie, so she thought it was a good bargain.

Ebenezer snatched it out of her fingers and rubbed... *Kazoom!* The genie appeared. "Take me and this palace far away!" shouted Ebenezer.

When Aladdin came home, he found only a patch of flattened earth. "Badra!" he cried. He wrung his hands in despair – and accidentally rubbed the carved brass ring he still wore.

Kazam! A wispy figure hovered before him. "I am the Genie of the Ring."

"Please, bring back my wife," begged Aladdin.

"I can't," said the genie. "My magic isn't as strong as that of the lamp. But I can take you to her."

The genie snapped his fingers, and Aladdin was in the stolen palace. As soon as he and Badra had finished hugging, they began to plan their escape...

That evening, Badra offered Ebenezer a drink. He swallowed it in two gulps and fell fast asleep, for it was laced with sleeping potion. Then Badra took the lamp from his pocket and tiptoed out, to where Aladdin was waiting.

Aladdin rubbed his ring. *Kazam!* "Carry Ebenezer to the cave under the mountain," he told the genie, "and lock him up!"

Badra rubbed the lamp. *Kazoom!* "Now, please take us home," she said.

With a smile, the genie did. And this time, without a wicked magician to spoil things, they lived happily ever after.

The Three Wishes

One fine day, an old man was out gathering mushrooms. He was about to pick an extra large one when he heard a tiny voice shout, "Please stop!"

The old man looked down – and blinked. There, peering out of the mushroom, was a fairy! She had made her home inside it.

"If you spare my mushroom, I will give you three wishes," she said.

The old man didn't think twice. "Thank you!" he cried, and hurried off to share the good news with his wife. "What should we wish for first?" he wondered. "A grand house, fancy clothes, a sack full of gold...?"

"You're early," said his wife, when she saw him. "Supper isn't ready yet."

"Oh," sighed the old man, feeling his tummy rumble. "I wish I had a nice sausage."

Ting! A fat, juicy sausage appeared on the table. His wife stared. "How did you do that?" So the old man explained...

"You silly man," cried his wife. "Wasting a wish on a sausage. I wish your sausage was on the end of your nose!"

Ting! The sausage dangled from the old man's nose.

"Oh no, I didn't mean it." She tried to pull the sausage off, but it wouldn't budge.

"Ow!"

"I'm sorry. Well, we still have one wish left. What will it be?"

The old man patted his sausage-nose gingerly. "I can't stay like this."

His wife nodded. "I wish that sausage was back on the table," she said. *Ting!* It was. "So much for our three wishes," she sighed. "But at least we'll have sausage for supper!"

Edited by Lesley Sims

Designed by Caroline Spatz

First published in 2013 by Usborne Publishing Ltd., Usborne House, 83-85 Saffron Hill,
London EC1N 8RT, England. www.usborne.com
Copyright © 2013 Usborne Publishing Ltd.